Aliens Love Dinopants

For Sheniz and Noah ~ C. F.

For Nia ~ B. C.

Originally published in Great Britain in 2015 by Simon & Schuster UK Ltd.

ISBN 978-1-338-16184-7

12 11 10 9 8 7 6 5 4 3 2 1   17 18 19 20 21 22

Printed in the U.S.A.   08

This edition first printing, January 2017

Designed by Karina Granda

• The Underpants Books •

Aliens Love Dinopants

ILLUSTRATED BY
Ben Cort

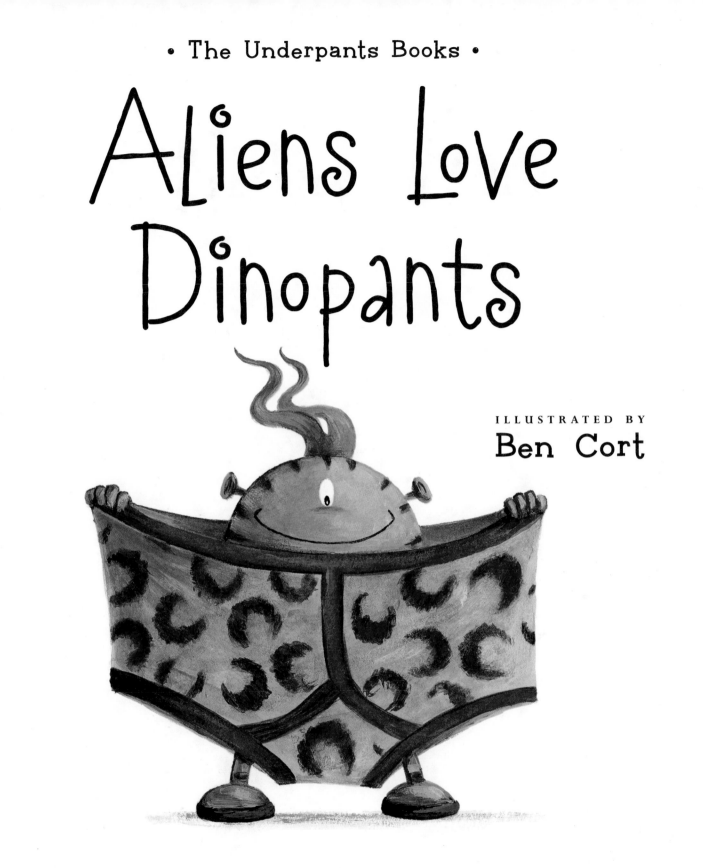

CLAIRE FREEDMAN

SCHOLASTIC INC.

A band of pants-mad aliens
Zoomed down here, when SURPRISE!
Bright lightning hit their spaceship, *BANG!*
And hurled them from the skies.

Crash-landing in thick jungle,

"Whoops!" the aliens gasped. "Oh dear!"

But their pants-tracker was BLEEPING.

How could underpants be here?

The aliens trekked through tangly trees,
The signal getting stronger.
Through slimy swamps, down deep ravines,
Could they go on much longer?

Their tracker just went BONKERS!

"Wow! We must be close," they cried.

It led them to a hidden gate.

"Let's take a peek inside!"

BLEEP! BLEEP! YIPPEE!

They'd found them!

(Those aliens are so clever!)

A stash of such gigantic undies,

Each pair could stretch forever!

"We'll take these pants!" the aliens laughed.

But . . . *RAAAAR!* They heard loud roars!

And found themselves surrounded by . . .

Ginormous dinosaurs!

The dinosaurs were furious.
"Hands off our drawers!"
they roared.
"We'll fight you pesky aliens,
To save our precious hoard!"

The aliens almost fainted!

"DINOSAURS? This can't be so!

You dinos were wiped out from Earth.

Pants-zillion years ago!"

"We hid down here," the dinos said.

"The humans didn't see!

We saved our pants.

but couldn't come out.

We wish we could roam free!"

"We ALL love pants," one alien cheered,
"So there's no need to fight!
I have a plan to get you out
And save you from your plight!"

Those busy aliens got to work,
With laser tools and saws.
They hammered, welded, chopped, and drilled,
Helped by the dinosaurs.

"TA-DA! A super dino-pod
To launch you into space!
We'll take you to our planet.
ZOOM! A most pants-tastic place!"

"Our new home's great!" the dinos said.
"There's underpants for all!"
It's fun the games that can be played
With pants both HUGE and small.

So when your laundry's on the line,
Quick! Guard it on the double.
With aliens AND dinosaurs,
There's twice pants-stealing trouble!